# Dear Parents:

Congratulations! Your child is taking the first steps on an exciting journey. The destination? Independent reading!

**STEP INTO READING**® will help your child get there. The program offers five steps to reading success. Each step includes fun stories and colorful art or photographs. In addition to original fiction and books with favorite characters, there are Step into Reading Non-Fiction Readers, Phonics Readers and Boxed Sets, Sticker Readers, and Comic Readers—a complete literacy program with something to interest every child.

## Learning to Read, Step by Step!

### Ready to Read    Preschool–Kindergarten
• big type and easy words • rhyme and rhythm • picture clues
For children who know the alphabet and are eager to begin reading.

### Reading with Help    Preschool–Grade 1
• basic vocabulary • short sentences • simple stories
For children who recognize familiar words and sound out new words with help.

### Reading on Your Own    Grades 1–3
• engaging characters • easy-to-follow plots • popular topics
For children who are ready to read on their own.

### Reading Paragraphs    Grades 2–3
• challenging vocabulary • short paragraphs • exciting stories
For newly independent readers who read simple sentences with confidence.

### Ready for Chapters    Grades 2–4
• chapters • longer paragraphs • full-color art
For children who want to take the plunge into chapter books but still like colorful pictures.

**STEP INTO READING**® is designed to give every child a successful reading experience. The grade levels are only guides; children will progress through the steps at their own speed, developing confidence in their reading. The F&P Text Level on the back cover serves as another tool to help you choose the right book for your child.

Remember, a lifetime love of reading starts with a single step!

Step into Reading, Random House, and the Random House colophon are registered trademarks
of Penguin Random House LLC.

Visit us on the Web!
StepIntoReading.com
randomhousekids.com

Educators and librarians, for a variety of teaching tools, visit us at
RHTeachersLibrarians.com

*Library of Congress Cataloging-in-Publication Data*
Berenstain, Stan.
The Berenstain bears ride the thunderbolt / The Berenstains.
    p. cm. — (Step into reading. A step 1 book)
Summary: The Bear family goes on a roller coaster ride.
ISBN 978-0-679-88718-8 (trade) — ISBN 978-0-679-98718-5 (lib. bdg.) —
ISBN 978-0-553-53699-7 (ebook)
[1. Roller coasters—Fiction. 2. Bears—Fiction.]
I. Berenstain, Jan. II. Title. III. Series: Step into reading. Step 1 book.
PZ7.B4483 Bff 2003 [E]—dc21 2002013649

Printed in the United States of America   30 29 28 27 26 25 24 23 22 21

# *The Berenstain Bears*
## *RIDE THE*

## The Berenstains

Random House 🏠 New York

# The Thunderbolt!

# Waiting in line.

# Buying tickets.

# Getting on.

Buckling up.

Going up.

Up, up, up!

Clickety-clickety

clackety-click!

# At the top.

Going down.

Down, down, down!

Clackety-clackety

clickety-clack!

# Down and around!

Upside down!

# Into the dark!

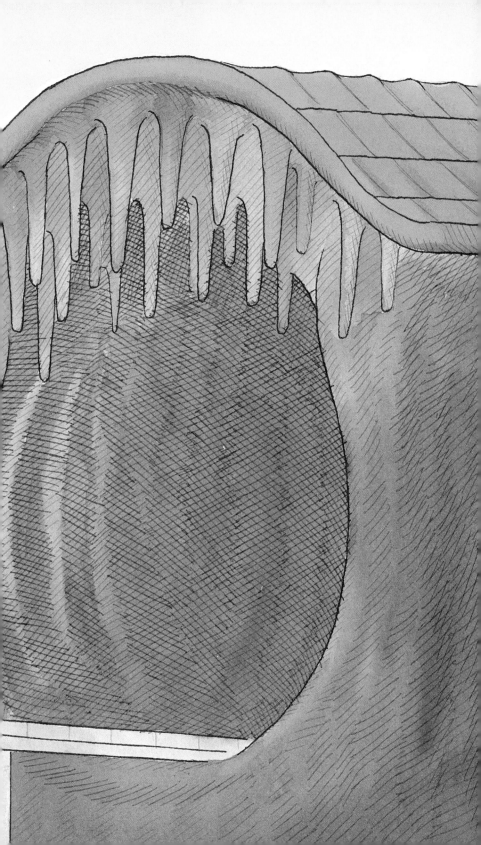

# Into the light.

Slowing down.

# Getting off.

"Again! Again!
Do it again!"

"Not so quick!
Not so quick!
Your papa looks
a little sick."

"But that was fun!

That was fun!"

Going on again,

minus one.